W9-ARX-720

MARC BROWN

ARTHUR

Chapter Books 4-6

Read all the
Marc Brown Arthur Chapter Books!

Chapter Books 4-6

Arthur and the Crunch Cereal Contest

Arthur Accused!

Locked in the Library!

Text by Stephen Krensky

Based on teleplays by Peter Hirsch,
James Greenberg, and Kathy Waugh

Little, Brown and Company

Boston   New York   London

Text has been reviewed by Laurel S. Ernst, M.A., Teachers College,
Columbia University, New York, New York; reading specialist,
Chappaqua, New York

Little, Brown originally published *Arthur and the Crunch Cereal
Contest* (1998), *Arthur Accused!* (1998), and *Locked in
the Library!* (1998) as individual chapter books.

ISBN 0-316-07595-7
LCCN 2001096578

10 9 8 7 6 5 4 3 2 1

WOR

Printed in the United States of America

For the best home team ever:
Pamela Dixon, Tolon Brown, Sheila Brown,
Linda Turrell, Rachel Breinin,
and Kevin O'Keeffe

Contents

• • • • • • • • • •

Arthur and the Crunch Cereal Contest

Chapter 1

. . . .

"A touch of cinnamon . . . a hint of brown sugar . . . just a suspicion of cloves."

Mr. Read stood in front of the kitchen stove, bringing his latest creation to life. The steam from the pot swirled up toward the frosted window.

"Yes, siree, on a chilly morning like this, everyone needs some oatmeal that will really stick to your ribs."

He swiveled around quickly, presenting a steaming pot.

The rest of the family was sitting at the table.

"I'm not very hungry this morning," said Arthur.

"Me, neither," said D.W.

Only baby Kate looked pleased. She liked playing with oatmeal. It always ended up in the most interesting places.

"Now, now," said their mother. "Your father's been working hard on this. Let's give it a chance."

"Thank you, dear," said Mr. Read. "And in recognition of your support, we'll start with a nice healthy portion for you."

He tilted the pot and tried to spoon some into her bowl. But nothing came out. The oatmeal had hardened like cement.

"Hmmm . . ." Mr. Read looked puzzled. "The baking soda must have reacted with the molasses. . . ."

"Oh, that's terrible!" said Mrs. Read. From the look on her face, though, it didn't appear as if she minded at all.

"That was *close*," whispered D.W.

Arthur nodded.

"Looks like we'll have to make do with regular cereal," said Mrs. Read. "Arthur, would you—"

"Sure, Mom!" Arthur got up to get the cereal from the cabinet.

Mr. Read put the pot in the sink. "We'll have to bury this later—with full military honors, of course."

Arthur opened the box of Crunch cereal. It was his favorite.

His father shook his head. "I don't understand the appeal of that sugar-coated cardboard. Believe me, all you'll get from that stuff is a mouthful of cavities."

"We're willing to take that risk," said D.W.

As Arthur shook out a serving, an envelope fell out of the box into his bowl.

"Wow!" said D.W. "And I thought letters only came in alphabet soup."

Arthur opened the envelope and read the note inside aloud.

"Welcome to the Crunch Cereal Jingle Contest. Send us your song — and you could win a year's supply of Crunch cereal."

Mr. Read shook his head. "I'll bet second place is a two-year supply."

Arthur kept reading.

"The winning jingle will also be aired on TV in the new Crunch cereal commercial. So don't just stand there, start crunching."

"If we won that contest," said D.W., "we'd be famous!"

"There's something here in the small print," said Arthur. " 'Include twenty box-tops with each entry.' " He sighed. "That's a lot of crunching."

"Isn't there something about 'Void where prohibited by law'?" asked Mr. Read.

Arthur looked. "I don't think so," he said.

"Good," said D.W.

Arthur dumped some cereal in her bowl. "I'm glad you feel that way. If you want to be famous, start eating."

Chapter 2

Over the next few days, Arthur thought about jingles while brushing his teeth.

Crunch, crunch.

He thought about them while taking a bath.

Crunch, crunch, crunch.

He even thought about them while doing his homework.

Crunch, crunch, crunch, crunch.

But none of this thinking got him very far. Wanting to write a jingle was a lot easier than actually making one up.

"Arthur, you need to get some fresh air," said his mother. "Go outside and play."

"I can't, Mom. The deadline is getting closer."

"Sometimes, it's good to take a break," said Mrs. Read. "Recharge your creative batteries. Clear your head. Why don't you go make a snowman?"

"I don't think—"

"Move it," said his mother. "That's an order."

Arthur went outside, but he wasn't happy about it. He started rolling a giant snowball. Then he started chipping pieces out of it.

The snowball was beginning to look like a giant piece of Crunch cereal.

"Is that what I think it is?"

D.W. had come outside, too. She shook her head at Arthur's snow sculpture.

"Mom wants me to clear my head," he explained. "I was hoping this would help."

"You're in a rut, Arthur," said D.W. "You need to think harder."

"I'm trying," Arthur insisted. "I've never thought so hard in my life."

"Well, it doesn't show much. Maybe I could help."

"We've been over this, D.W. You have your job."

"I know, I know. I'm supposed to eat the cereal."

Arthur nodded. "Don't forget that."

"Forget it?" said D.W. "How could I? You put boxes in my bed, my toy chest, and my closet. Everywhere I go, Crunch cereal is waiting for me."

"Don't complain," said Arthur. "I'm eating it, too. And I've still got the hard part to deal with."

D.W. was not impressed. "You don't seem to be dealing very well. Have you tried *dunce?* That sort of rhymes with *crunch.*"

12

"Sort of? I don't think the Crunch cereal people are looking for *sort of*. They're looking for rhythm. They're looking for poetry —"

"They're looking for a way to sell more cereal," said D.W.

Arthur shook his head. "You just don't have the right attitude. It's not surprising. You're too young to understand great art."

D.W. laughed. "I may not know great art, but I know what I like."

"We're not talking about ice cream flavors here, D.W. A jingle has to be the perfect combination of words with the perfect melody."

"Well, what about *lunch?*" said D.W. "That rhymes with *crunch*."

Arthur looked up at the sky and sighed. Why couldn't inspiration hit him like a flash of lightning? He was ready. He was waiting.

A snowball hit him in the chest.

"Bull's-eye!" cried D.W.

"I'll bull's-eye you right back," said Arthur.

He scooped up some snow and threw it back.

For that moment, at least, his head was clear.

Chapter 3

· · · · · · · · · · · ·

The school music room was empty except for Arthur. All the other kids were out at recess, running around and playing in the snow.

Arthur was trying out notes at the piano.

Dooonnng!

Too low, thought Arthur. Too sad.

He tried a high note.

Diiiiink.

Too silly, thought Arthur.

He played a note in between.

Diiinnnng.

Arthur nodded. It was a start.

The door to the music room banged open.

"How's your jingle coming, Arthur?" asked Buster. His face was red. Melting snow was dripping off his coat.

"I've pretty much finished the words."

"Let's hear them," said Buster.

Arthur cleared his throat.

"Eat Crunch," he said.

Buster waited. But Arthur seemed to be done.

"Is there more?" he asked.

"No, that's it," said Arthur. "What do you think?"

Buster thought it over. "It's short," he decided.

"Short and sweet," said Arthur. "Just like the cereal."

"Makes sense to me," said Buster. "I like it. So can you come out and play now?"

"I need more than words," said Arthur.

"I need a tune to go with it. But I haven't had much luck. . . ."

"Hmmmm," said Buster. He looked at Arthur sitting alone at the piano. "Maybe you should think bigger."

"What would be bigger?"

"You know, more people, more instruments."

Arthur liked the idea.

"If you had more musicians," Buster went on, "it would be easy to come up with a tune."

"More musicians?" said Arthur. "You mean, like a band?"

"You can have auditions and everything," said Buster. "We could check on the playground. I'll bet lots of kids would be interested."

Arthur grabbed his coat. "Okay," he said. "Let's find out."

The school yard was filled with

bundled-up kids running around and making a lot of noise.

"Hi, Francine!" said Buster.

She was standing over a fallen pile of snow.

"It would have been beautiful," she sighed.

"Arthur has a question for you," said Buster.

"The snow sculpture to end all snow sculptures. It was bold. It was daring."

"I was wondering, Francine . . . ," Arthur began.

"But I couldn't do it by myself. I needed the help of my friends. And were they here for me?" She looked up at Arthur and Buster. "No, they were inside doing some dumb thing instead." She folded her arms. "I don't think I'll ever be able to forgive them."

"That's too bad," said Arthur. "Come

on, Buster, we don't want to ask her at a time like this. She's in too much pain."

"Ask me? Ask me what?"

"Arthur wants you to be in his band," said Buster.

Francine's eyes widened. "A band? I get to play my drums?"

"You would," said Arthur. "But since you're feeling so bad . . ."

Francine looked back at the fallen pile of snow. She gave it a kick. "Oh, well," she said. "Easy come, easy go." She turned back to Arthur.

"So, when do we start?"

Chapter 4

• • • • • • • • • • • •

Arthur walked to the middle of the huge con-cert hall and stared out at the lights. He knew the audience was there, even if he couldn't see them. These were the country's greatest music critics. They had all come to hear his band play the Crunch cereal jingle.

Arthur spoke into the microphone. "Ladies and gentlemen, there's been a change in the program," he announced. "As you can see, I don't have a complete band yet. But Buster, Francine, and I will gladly—"

The audience started to boo. They had flown in from all over the country to hear the full band, not a few instruments patched together.

"Don't waste our time!"

"Get off the stage!"

"Come back when you're really ready!"

Arthur held up his hands. "If I could just explain . . . ," he began.

"Hey, Arthur!" said Buster. "Snap out of it!"

Arthur blinked. He looked around his living room. "I'm snapping, I'm snapping," he said.

"What's the matter?" Buster asked. "You look worried."

"Well, I am, a little. What if nobody comes today? What if they just ignored my signs about auditioning?"

"Um, Arthur, I don't think that will be a problem. Look!"

Outside the Read garage, a long line of kids had formed. Each of them was holding an instrument.

"Great!" said Arthur. "Let's get started.

As Buster took charge of the line,

Mr. Read came out to see what was going on.

Buster explained why all the kids were there.

Mr. Read looked relieved. "Oh, it's that cereal business. Well, this is certainly ambitious." He paused. "Are we expected to feed everyone?"

"Oh, no," said Buster. "Arthur has that all taken care of."

Inside the garage, Arthur had put out bowls of Crunch cereal.

"Eat up, eat up!" he said. "There's plenty for everyone."

After a few minutes of crunching, the auditions began.

Sue Ellen was first. She played a riff of notes on her saxophone.

"Good," said Arthur. "But did I hear something rattling?"

"I think some of the Crunch cereal fell into my horn."

"Well, try and blow it out. Next!"

Arthur listened to kids with banjos and piccolos, oboes and kazoos. One kid blew such a long note on his trumpet that he almost fainted.

The best part was when Grandma Thora arrived.

"Heard about the tryouts," she said. "No special treatment for me. Don't even think about all the cookies I've baked over the years. And never mind about the chicken soup, either. Just listen up."

And with that, she pulled out a harmonica and began to play.

The jazzy notes drew everyone's attention. And then she sang: "Grandma's got a brand-new bag! Gonna groove it all night long. . . ."

Arthur was impressed. "You're hired!" he said.

The last person in line was Binky Barnes.

"You ready?" he asked.

Arthur nodded.

"Solo for clarinet by some old dead guy."

Binky played a complicated series of notes.

Arthur's mouth dropped open.

"Wow!" said Buster. "That was beautiful!"

Binky stalked up to him. "Yeah, yeah, yeah . . . So am I in or not?"

"Absolutely!" said Arthur. "Well, on one condition . . ."

"Which is?"

"That you help me finish the last box of Crunch."

Binky smiled. "It's a deal," he said.

Chapter 5

. . . .

Arthur stood in front of the newly formed Crunch Bunch band. Besides Buster and Francine, it included Binky, Muffy, the Brain, Sue Ellen, Prunella, and Grandma Thora.

"Where should *I* go?" D.W. asked.

She was standing by the door.

Arthur walked over to her. "Auditions are over, D.W. Besides, you don't even play an instrument."

"Don't worry. I don't want to play. I just want to be in charge."

"That position is filled," Arthur said firmly. He opened the door. "I think I hear

Nadine calling you." Nadine was D.W.'s invisible friend. "She sounds like she's stuck in a snowbank. You'd better check."

"Hmmph!" muttered D.W. "Big brothers can be so bossy."

Arthur closed the door behind her and walked back to the others.

"Now, where were we? Oh, yes . . . I want to start off with a bang. So everyone should play a real loud note. Then I'll—"

"Could we—," Francine began.

Arthur stared at her. "Excuse me. Does someone have a question? I don't see anyone raising a hand."

Francine rolled her eyes and raised her hand.

"Yes, Francine?"

"I just thought it might be nice to start off with a drum roll. For dramatic impact."

"Yeah," said Muffy, putting her violin under her chin. "Followed by some strings."

She started playing, and the Brain started plucking his cello.

"Then we'll add the horns," said Sue Ellen.

She blew into her saxophone while Prunella raised her trumpet.

"No," said Arthur.

Everyone kept playing.

Arthur waved his arms. "No! NO! *NO! NOOOOO!*"

Everyone stopped. The silence was deafening.

"Listen to me," said Arthur. "I got the entry form. I've eaten fifteen boxes of Crunch, and this is *my* jingle. So we're going to play it *my* way! Any questions?"

"Nope."

"None from me."

"Very clear."

"Carry on."

Arthur took a deep breath. "Good," he said.

"But what do we play from?" asked the Brain.

"I'll show you," said Arthur.

He passed out some sheet music.

"There isn't much here," said Francine. "Just a few notes."

"Well, it's a jingle," said Arthur. "The notes repeat. Now, if everyone's ready, let's give it everything we've got. One, two, and—"

Arthur motioned the band to play.

And they did.

WHRAMMMPAARROOOOO!

The strange sound shot out of Arthur's garage in all directions.

It hit Mrs. Tibble first. She was walking along the sidewalk. The sound shook the snow from the branches overhead, covering her like powdered sugar on a doughnut.

At the same time, Bob the barber was cutting Miss Tingley's hair.

WHRAMMMPAARROOOOO!

The sound blasted through the closed windows. Bob was startled — and clipped off most of her bangs.

The sound weakened at the edge of town, but it still packed a punch. Muffy's parents, the Crosswires, heard it in their living room.

Whrammmpaarrooooo!

"It's an air raid," said Ed.

"We don't have air raids," his wife, Millicent, reminded him.

"Well, I'm not taking any chances. We spent all that money on a bomb shelter. We may as well use it."

And they both went down to the basement — where there was nothing more to be heard.

Chapter 6

Inside Arthur's garage, everyone stared at one another. Their mouths were wide open.

"Well," said Arthur, "maybe that was too much of a bang. But I think it's a good start."

There was a knock on the garage door. Arthur opened it.

A police officer was standing outside. Her cruiser was out on the street. The lights were flashing.

"Oh, my," said Arthur.

"I'm investigating a complaint," said

the officer. "Actually, we had a number of calls."

"You did?" said Arthur. "What about?"

The officer looked at her notes. "Someone thought a cat was being tortured. We take a pretty dim view of that around here. Do you have a cat?"

"No cats," said Arthur. "Just a dog. And he's fine. Honest."

"Someone else heard the siren warning of a nuclear meltdown." The officer looked over Arthur's shoulder. "You're not using any unauthorized materials in here, are you? No uranium? No fancy isotopes?"

Arthur shook his head. "We were just rehearsing a jingle."

The officer scanned the band members. "All right, then." She put away her pad. "Everything seems to be in order. But just a word of advice . . ."

"Yes, officer."

"Keep the volume down. Try not to let your jingle *jangle* — if you know what I mean."

Arthur nodded. "I do, officer. Thank you, officer. Good-bye."

He shut the door behind her.

"That was close," said Buster.

Binky was looking out the window. "She turned off the flashing lights. Too bad. Still, we might make the newspaper this week."

Arthur turned back to the others. Everyone was packing up.

"Hey! Wait! What are you doing? We'll get the tune right! Don't give up!"

"We don't want to be arrested," said Sue Ellen.

"And I'm very busy. I am *not* building jail time into my calendar," said Muffy.

"But the contest . . ."

The Brain sidestepped Arthur with his cello.

"We're all going home for lunch," said Prunella.

Francine looked at him. "We'll come back later. I just hope you're inspired while we're gone."

"*Very* inspired," Muffy added.

Grandma Thora got her coat. "Don't get discouraged, dear. It's a bit hard on the ears so far, but I'm sure you can fix that."

The rest of the band filed out.

Arthur watched them leave. Only Buster was left.

"You'll feel better after lunch," he said. "I know I always think better on a full stomach."

Arthur's stomach was in a big knot.

"I can't think about food right now. I have work to do."

He moved toward the house.

"You should take a break, though," said Buster.

Arthur spun around.

"Did Mozart take breaks?"

Buster didn't know. He couldn't even spell Mozart, much less comment on his schedule.

"Did the guy who wrote 'Ring-Around-the-Rosey' take breaks? I don't think so. They were dedicated. They were committed. And so am I."

Chapter 7

· · · · · · · · · · · ·

The knot in Arthur's stomach did not go away. It just sat there, tight and uncomfortable. Arthur tried to ignore it. He sat in his living room hunched over the piano. He stared at the keys.

The keys seemed to stare back.

Arthur played one note.

Diinnnnng.

Arthur wanted to play another. But he hesitated. There were so many notes to choose from.

"Eat Crunch," sang Arthur. He groaned. "It's good, but it isn't enough. I'll never come up with anything more."

His head fell forward on the keys, causing a jumble of chords to fill the air.

It was dark with his eyes closed. He opened them slowly. He could barely see through the gloom.

The fog parted up ahead, revealing a creaky bridge. It was strung with rope and wooden planks. The planks were painted white and black — like the keys of a piano. They swayed in the wind.

That bridge doesn't look too secure, thought Arthur. But it was the only way over the mountain pass.

D.W. was standing on the other side.

"If you want to cross safely," she said, "you have to play the right notes."

"Okay," said Arthur. "But what are they?"

His sister laughed. "You'll find out," she said. "One way or the other."

Arthur frowned. He took a leap forward, landing on the third plank.

Donnng!

*"That's one small step for Arthur," said
D.W. "Keep it up."*

Arthur jumped to a black plank.

Dinnng!

"Two for two," said D.W.

*Arthur felt better. Maybe this wouldn't be so
hard. He walked onto the very next plank.*

Craaccck!

Uh-oh, thought Arthur.

*As he fell through the bridge, he could hear
D.W. humming. Why couldn't she have
hummed that tune earlier? It was catchy. It
had a good beat. He could have played it right
across the bridge.*

Arthur jerked his head up. The bridge
was gone. So was the mountain pass. He
was back facing the piano.

But D.W. was still humming.

Arthur followed the sound into the hall.
It was coming from upstairs.

Arthur tiptoed up the steps to D.W.'s
room. He peeked inside.

His sister was sitting on her bed, brushing Nadine's hair. Arthur could tell that even though he couldn't see Nadine. Only D.W. could see her.

As D.W. brushed, she started to sing:

> *"Oh, I have a hunch*
> *Breakfast, dinner, and lunch*
> *Would be so fun to munch,*
> *If I had it with Nadine!"*

It was the same song she had been humming before, only now she had added the words.

Arthur's eyes bulged. It was all there right in front of him. All he had to do was change the Nadine part.

"Perfect! Just PERFECT!"

He raced back downstairs.

D.W. looked at the spot where Arthur had been standing.

"Was that Arthur?" asked Nadine.

"I think so."

"He's definitely lost his mind," said Nadine. "Too much of that cereal. What's it called again?"

"Crunch," said D.W.

"If you ask me," said Nadine, "he's crunched till he's out to lunch."

They both laughed.

Chapter 8

The mood was grim in Arthur's garage as the band members returned from lunch. The sun was shining outside, but the garage itself seemed darkened by a cloud.

Francine was tapping out a slow march on her drums.

Muffy was warming up with some painful screeches on her violin. They sounded as if she had accidentally stepped on a cat's tail.

Binky was putting a new reed in his clarinet. "I hope everyone ate a big lunch," he said. "I know I did. It could be a very long afternoon."

Even Grandma Thora seemed a little down. She was tapping her foot and singing to herself.

"Time is quickly running out,
And Arthur's on the spot,
He must put aside all doubt,
And show us what he's got."

After each line, she wailed softly on her harmonica.

"Cheer up, everyone," said Buster. "I'm sure Arthur won't let us down."

"He might not want to," said Prunella. "But eating all that Crunch cereal may have rotted his brain."

Francine made a face. "If it starts oozing out his ears, I'm out of here."

At that moment Arthur rushed in. His brain didn't look rotted, at least from the outside. In fact, he looked pretty happy.

"I've got it, everybody! I've got the jingle. Listen to this!"

The room grew still.

Arthur started to sing.

"Oh, I have a hunch
  Breakfast, dinner, and lunch
  Would be so fun to munch,
  If I had it with some . . . CRUNCH!"

"It's got a good beat," said Grandma Thora, snapping her fingers. "And you can dance to it."

Buster clapped. "Way to go, Arthur!"

"Amazing!" said Francine. "That actually was . . ."

"Good," Muffy finished for her.

"What inspired you?" asked the Brain.

"It's hard to explain inspiration," said Arthur. "I was sitting in the living room. And I heard this tune . . ."

Arthur paused. He suddenly remembered where all his inspiration had come
from. He lowered his eyes and fiddled
with his glasses.

"I, uh, heard this tune in my head. And
then . . . and then the words just came to
me. That's all."

Buster was impressed. "Wow! I guess
that's how a great jingle is born. Nothing
at first . . . Nothing at second, either. And
then, poof, out of nowhere — something
beautiful."

"I guess so," said Sue Ellen.

"I've heard worse, I suppose," said
Binky.

"Good for you, Arthur," said Grandma
Thora.

Arthur bit his lip. "Well, I'm glad everyone likes it. Now we just have to play our
parts."

He handed out some sheet music.

"We can all play and sing this together."

He grinned. "And if you want to add a little something, go right ahead."

They practiced for a few minutes. Everyone seemed pretty comfortable.

Arthur set up his tape recorder.

"Ready?" he asked.

Everyone nodded.

Arthur pushed the *record* button.

They played the song through—but not too loudly. Arthur shut his eyes and sang out loud and strong. When he opened his eyes, he noticed Pal jumping up and down in the yard.

It was a good sign, he thought.

Chapter 9

. . . .

Once the tape was ready, Arthur couldn't wait to get it into the mail. He sent the band home with his promise to let everyone know as soon as he heard anything.

"We're going to be rich!" said Buster.

Arthur shook his head. "Um, Buster, the prize doesn't include any money."

"Oh, well, we'll be famous, then. I can be flexible."

He tooted twice on his tuba and headed for home.

Arthur went into the house to get the package ready. He wrote a quick letter and put it in an envelope with the tape.

Grandma Thora helped him figure out how many stamps he needed.

Then he went back outside.

"Where are you going, Arthur?" asked D.W.

She and Nadine were playing in the snow.

"Can't talk now, D.W. I'm in a hurry."

His sister spotted the package under his arm. "Ooooh! Is that the jingle for the contest? I heard you playing something before."

Arthur looked down at the package.

"This? Oh, yes, I guess so."

"So, what did you come up with? Let's hear it."

"You don't have to be polite, D.W. I know you and Nadine aren't interested."

"Nadine doesn't like it when you put words in her mouth, Arthur. She likes to decide things for herself."

"Good for her," said Arthur. "But, really, I'm in a—"

D.W. frowned. "You like the song, don't you?"

"Oh, yes. Very much."

"Well, sing it to me."

"Oh . . . munch . . . crunch . . . snap, crackle, pop . . . something like that. Oops, look at the time. I don't want to miss the last mail pick-up."

D.W. would have said more, but Arthur was no longer there to hear it.

D.W. turned back to Nadine. Sometimes her brother was more than a little strange. She shrugged, hoping it wasn't contagious.

As Arthur headed down the street, he slowed to a walk. He had avoided telling D.W. where the jingle had come from. Of course, she didn't even know she had helped him. So there was no reason to tell her. Not really. Great artists were always taking inspiration from the people and places around them.

Arthur was on the stage in a concert setting in the park. He was sitting in front of a piano. A cheering crowd could be heard in the background. He played the theme to the jingle and flashed a big grin. The crowd cheered.

Many rows back, D.W. was pushing her way to the stage.

"Arthur! Arthur! I know that song. Did you tell them the truth?"

Arthur heard his sister's voice but couldn't see her.

"D.W., where are you?"

D.W. had almost reached the stage, but before she could climb the stairs, several people rushed forward to block her way.

"Who was that?" asked the beefy head of security.

"Oh, just one of my many fans," said

Arthur. "Some of them can be very deter-mined."

Arthur sighed. He had arrived at the mailbox. All he had to do was drop in the envelope. Just pull down the handle, and drop it in. Nothing to it, really. But somehow he couldn't. Not yet. He just stood there, blinking in the sunlight.

Chapter 10

On Saturday morning two weeks later, D.W. and Arthur were watching TV in their pajamas.

"Will the Bionic Bunny be able to defeat Captain Junk Food? We'll find out after these commercial messages."

"Captain Junk Food is pretty powerful," said D.W. "I think the Bionic Bunny has his hands full."

"Could be," said Arthur. "And the show is making me hungry."

He headed for the kitchen—but stopped suddenly as a song came from the TV.

*"Oh, I have a hunch
Breakfast, dinner, and lunch . . ."*

Arthur turned to see a Crunch nugget in a tuxedo singing into a microphone.

*"Would be so fun to munch
If I had it with some . . . CRUNCH!"*

D.W. yawned. "This commercial isn't as good as the old one — hey, wait a minute. . . ."

Arthur raced to the TV and stood in front of it.

"D.W., I can explain everything."

His sister folded her arms. "You better," she said.

"Calm down in there," said their father, poking his head out from the kitchen. "Breakfast is ready. It's my special oatmeal. Fiber is its middle name."

D.W. shut off the TV and headed for the kitchen. Arthur followed.

The table was set with bowls of industrial-strength oatmeal.

"You see," said Arthur, "I was going to tell you. I mean, at first I wasn't. But I never mailed that entry. I did it over. But I still didn't tell you. . . . I was convinced I'd lose—I mean, you'd lose."

D.W. rolled her eyes. "Arthur, you're making even less sense than usual. What's going on?"

"You'll love this stuff," said Mr. Read. "One bowl—and you won't be hungry till dinner."

He tapped the oatmeal with a spoon.

"In fact, you may not even be able to move till dinner."

"The contest!" Arthur went on. "I didn't tell you because—"

"Tell me what?"

"That I—"

He was interrupted by the doorbell.

"Who could that be?" said Mr. Read.

He went to the front door and opened it. A delivery man stood outside. He was wearing a hat shaped like a bowl of cereal.

"Is this the Read residence?"

"Yes?" Mr. Read said cautiously.

The man cleared his throat. "On behalf of the Crunch Cereal Company, I am happy to present you with a year's supply of Crunch cereal."

He motioned to his partner, who dropped a huge crate of boxes onto the Reads' driveway.

"We also have a certificate proclaiming the winner of the Crunch Cereal Jingle Contest."

Mr. Read looked overwhelmed. "And that is?"

"Ms. D.W. Read."

"Me?" said D.W.

Arthur sighed. "That's what I was trying to tell you."

A little later the whole family was gathered outside.

"I wanted to tell you that I sent your song in," said Arthur. "But I didn't want you to get your hopes up. You aren't mad, are you?"

D.W. just laughed. "You sent that crummy thing in? And it won?" She beamed. "Of course, I have much better songs than that!"

"Oh, really?" said Arthur. "Such as?"

D.W. smiled. "Well, there's the one I wrote this morning:

> *Oh, everyone thinks*
> *that my brother stinks*
> *like a piece of yellow cheese!*
> *But me, I say*
> *that he's okay*
> *as long as there's a breeze."*

"D.W.!"

Her sister started to run. Arthur chased after her.

"Come back here," he said. "I'll show you who stinks. But don't step on the cereal."

"Moooom."

"Daaaad!"

Their parents sighed.

"Who's going to eat all this cereal?" asked Mr. Read.

Mrs. Read pointed to Arthur and D.W., who were now pelting each other with snowballs. "They will. Don't you see? They're working on their appetites."

"Oh," said Mr. Read. "In that case, let's leave them to it."

Then they both went back inside, closing the door firmly behind them.

Arthur Accused!

Chapter 1

• • • • • • • • • •

Hello, stranger. I'm Buster Baxter, private eye. You can call me Buster for short. I'm going to tell you about my first case. It involved my pal Arthur, some missing quarters, and a whole lot of trouble.

The whole thing started two days ago. It was an ordinary Wednesday — the kind that comes right between Tuesday and Thursday. The middle of the week, when anything can happen — and usually does.

The school day had just ended, and Arthur was standing in the school hallway behind a long table. In front of him was a bowl half-filled with quarters.

"Help the fire department buy a new puppy!" Arthur called. "Only a quarter!"

A couple of kids dropped in quarters.

"Thanks," said Arthur. "Thanks a lot."

Binky Barnes walked up to him. His head and shoulders blocked the light from the hall window. "What's with the bowl, Arthur?"

"I'm collecting money for Mrs. MacGrady's fund drive. We're going to buy a puppy for the fire department." He showed Binky a picture.

"That dog has a lot of spots. You sure it isn't sick?"

"No, no. Dalmatians all look like that. So what do you think? How about a quarter?"

Binky considered it. He weighed the thought of a shiny quarter against a little dalmatian puppy. The puppy in his head

rolled over and made little snuffling sounds. It sat up and wagged its tail. The quarter just sat there being shiny.

"Here," said Binky. He reached into his pocket and flipped a quarter into the bowl. "There's just one thing," he added, glaring at Arthur.

"What's that?"

"Don't tell anybody I gave. It's bad for my image."

"Okay," said Arthur.

Binky seemed satisfied, at least for the moment.

"Hey, Arthur!" yelled Buster as he ran down the hall.

"What's with the goofy hat?" asked Arthur.

"This hat is not goofy," said Buster. "It's a fedora — part of my new detective kit. I've been snooping — ah, looking for crimes."

"Have you found any?"

"No." Buster pushed back the brim of his hat. "But I did pick up some secret information."

He peered to the left and right, making sure no one else was listening.

"You promise this will go no further?"

Arthur nodded.

Buster leaned forward. "Third-grade picnic this Friday," he whispered.

Arthur rolled his eyes. "I know that, Buster. There have been signs up for two weeks."

"Oh. Well, I was half right. It's still information. Anyway, I'm not giving up. I'll find a crime. Maybe I'll find one at the arcade. My mom's taking me there this afternoon. Want to come?"

Most of the kids seemed to have gone home. Arthur figured he had probably collected all the quarters he was going to get for the day. And the arcade was a great place.

"Sure," he said. "Just let me take these quarters to Mrs. MacGrady."

He emptied the quarters from the bowl into a paper bag.

"I'll go find my mom outside," said Buster. "We'll wait for you. Hurry!"

Arthur nodded and ran down the hall.

Chapter 2

I wasn't with Arthur for the next few minutes. Maybe if I had been, he wouldn't have had any problems. But as it says in the Detective's Handbook, *When life takes a wrong turn, just try not to get lost.*

Arthur hurried to the cafeteria kitchen. He could tell that Mr. Morris, the janitor, had cleaned the floors since lunch. "Clean enough to eat off of," Mr. Morris liked to say, but Arthur preferred plates.

Mrs. MacGrady was on the phone.

"What's that, Chief? Have you thought of a name yet?"

Arthur waved, trying to get her attention. He didn't want to keep Buster and his mother waiting.

But Mrs. MacGrady didn't see him.

"Smokey. Sure, that's a nice name for a dog. I see, I see . . ."

Arthur tried to be patient. On the counter next to him were some baking ingredients. There were bags of flour and sugar, sticks of butter, eggs, and chocolate squares.

"Where there's Smokey, there's a firefighter. Cute, Chief. Very cute. I just don't want the dog to get a complex. Dogs are sensitive, you know."

The bag was getting heavy in Arthur's hand. He went to put it down and accidentally knocked over the bag of flour.

"Chester's a fine name for a dog, don't you think? My first husband was named Chester."

Since Mrs. MacGrady still wasn't watching, Arthur was able to clean up the flour without her seeing him. Some of it had gotten into the bag of quarters, but that was okay because flour wouldn't do the quarters any harm.

Arthur looked at the clock. He had been standing there for more than five minutes.

"Mrs. MacGrady? Excuse me, Mrs. MacGrady?" He held up the bag of quarters.

She waved her hand, although whether she was waving to Arthur or making motions to the phone, it was hard to know.

"I'm just leaving —," Arthur began.

But Mrs. MacGrady, still talking on the phone, had turned away.

Arthur couldn't wait any longer. If he did, Buster would have a fit. Mrs. MacGrady was bound to be off the phone soon.

"I'm leaving the bag on the counter," Arthur called out. "Right here, next to the flour."

Then he left.

Chapter 3

• • • • • • • • • • •

When Arthur and I arrived at the arcade, I had two things on my mind. One was the games themselves. I wanted a return match with Alien Explorer, which had roughed me up the last time. That game needed to be taught a lesson. And I was just the one to do it.

The other thing on my mind was finding a mystery to solve. Arcades draw shifty characters the way a garbage dump draws flies. I figured something would come my way if I kept a good lookout.

"Buster," said Arthur, "what are you doing with that magnifying glass?"

"Just checking things out." Buster was peering closely at a table. "Some mysteries like to play hide-and-seek." He moved the glass back to Arthur, looking up and down. "Look at you, for example."

"What *about* me?" said Arthur.

"You've got white stuff on your clothes."

"I do not."

Buster looked closer. "Definitely some kind of powder."

Arthur looked down. There was a little . . . Suddenly he smiled. "Oh, that's no mystery. When I was dropping off the quarters in the cafeteria, I accidentally spilled some flour. It must have gotten on my shirt."

Buster looked disappointed. "Well, it *could* have been a mystery."

"Sorry," said Arthur. "Anyway, I thought we were here to play."

They made the rounds, playing some games themselves and watching others

play, too. Neither of them was very lucky at surviving *CrashCourse 2000* or getting through the night at *Haunted Hotel,* but Buster did better at *Alien Explorer.*

"Take that, you mangy mutant!" he cried. "Ah, revenge is sweet!" The mutant had always done him in before.

"Just a few more minutes, boys," Buster's mother called out to them. She was waiting for them outside the arcade.

Buster was out of money, but Arthur still had enough for one more game. He decided to try a pinball machine. He put in his quarters and pulled the knob. As he re-leased it, the ball shot up the slot and around the ramp.

"Go, Arthur, go!" said Buster, who never had much luck at pinball.

The ball ricocheted around the platform. Whenever it lost speed and fell down-ward, Arthur caught it with the flipper and sent it up again.

"Whoa! That was close, Arthur! Keep it up."

As Arthur's score rose, the machine lit up in more and more colors. A crowd began to gather behind him.

"Watch out, there!"

"Hold it . . . now!"

Arthur was on a roll.

"Go for the spinner!"

Arthur did his best, but finally the third ball dodged the right flipper and sank into the hole.

"Arthur, you did it!" cried Buster. "You hit the high score!"

Arthur looked up. His 868,233 points were in first place. He even got to put his initials next to them.

"That score will stand forever," said Buster. He pounded Arthur on the back as the onlookers cheered.

When they left the arcade, Buster was

still excited. "My best friend hit the high score," he said proudly to one and all.

It wasn't the same as finding a mystery to solve, but it was still pretty good.

Chapter 4

●●●●●●●●●●●●

As much as I hated to admit it, I was start-ing to feel a little down. Why was it so hard to find a mystery to investigate? Did all detec-tives have these problems? Still, at least I had some good news to share at school the next day.

"Step aside, everyone. Make way! Pinball wizard coming through."

Buster made these comments as he and Arthur walked down the hall.

"Buster, please!" said Arthur. "It's em-barrassing."

"Don't be so modest, Arthur. You deserve the attention."

Arthur sighed.

"Nimble fingers here! Eyes like a hawk. Reflexes like a cat!"

As they passed the principal's office, Mr. Haney waved them in.

"Good morning, Arthur, Buster," he said. "Oh, Arthur, don't forget to give Mrs. MacGrady the quarters you collected for her fund drive."

"I already did, Mr. Haney."

The school secretary, Miss Tingley, frowned. "That's odd. She told me she never got them."

"Aha!" said Buster. "Maybe they were stolen."

"Buster, please contain yourself," said Mr. Haney. The principal turned to Arthur. "Is it possible you brought them home by mistake?"

"No," said Buster. "He came straight to the arcade with me. In fact, he did very well at pinball. You're looking at Mr. High Score."

"Really?" Mr. Haney frowned. Miss Tingley frowned, too.

"I got the high score once," Buster went on. "Cost me a fortune. Took all my birthday money. Like a hundred quarters. Boy, did I —"

Buster stopped suddenly. He stared at Arthur. So did Mr. Haney and Miss Tingley.

"What's the matter?" asked Arthur.

"We have a little mystery here," said Mr. Haney.

Miss Tingley frowned again. "Not so little," she said.

A short while later, Arthur found himself sitting in the principal's office. He felt very small. The chair he was sitting in was very uncomfortable.

"You were responsible for the money," Mr. Haney was saying.

"You certainly were," Miss Tingley added.

Arthur shrank farther into the chair.

He looked from one stern face to the other. "You mean . . . you think *I* stole the quarters? But I left them on the cafeteria counter."

"Well, Mrs. MacGrady never saw them," Mr. Haney said. "You were responsible for them. If that money doesn't turn up, I'm afraid you'll have to serve a day —"

Miss Tingley cleared her throat.

"I mean, a week of after-school detention." Mr. Haney paused. "And no third-grade picnic for you tomorrow."

Arthur was horrified.

As he left the office, Buster rushed up to him.

"So what happened?"

Arthur explained it to him. "My first

important job, and everyone thinks I'm a thief. But I'm innocent."

"Of course you are," said Buster. "That's why you need a detective. Like, say . . . me."

"I don't know, Buster. Do you really think you can find out what happened to the quarters?"

"No problem! I could solve this case in my sleep. Well, no, I guess I'd have to be awake. And not wearing my pajamas, either. But don't worry, Arthur. Buster Baxter is on the case. You'll be going to that picnic tomorrow. Trust me."

Arthur wanted to believe him, but he wished he felt more hopeful. "Okay, Buster, do your stuff. But promise me one thing."

"Sure. What is it?"

"Try not to get me into any deeper trouble than I'm in now. Things are bad enough as it is."

Chapter 5

• • • • • • • • • • • •

In every case there's a key witness, and this case was no different. I knew who she was, and she knew who she was, too.

Last name: MacGrady.

First name: Mrs.

Occupation: Cafeteria lady.

Buster found Mrs. MacGrady in the cafeteria kitchen. She was mixing ingredients in a large bowl. He explained that he was investigating the disappearance of Arthur's quarters.

"Can you tell me your whereabouts yesterday afternoon?" he asked.

" 'Whereabouts,' huh? That's a pretty fancy way of asking me where I was. Well, I was right here in the kitchen, making brownies. Buster, keep your hands away from that bowl!"

"Aha!" said Buster, pulling back his hand. "Maybe I should taste this. It could be evidence."

Mrs. MacGrady waved a spatula at him. "Nice try. But you'll have to wait for the picnic like everyone else."

She moved over to a long table covered with tiny cherry tarts and began squirting whipped cream onto each one.

"I remember speaking to the chief. We had quite a long conversation. Then I made the brownies."

"Did you see Arthur?"

"No, I didn't see anyone all afternoon. Oh, wait, that's not true. Mr. Morris was here. My mixer jammed a few times, and the brownie mix overflowed onto the floor. He came in to mop up the mess."

"Hmmm," said Buster, popping one of the cherry tarts into his mouth.

"Maybe you should talk to Mr. Morris," Mrs. MacGrady suggested.

"Mank you fery huch," Buster mumbled, and ran out before she could say anything.

He found Mr. Morris, the school janitor, pushing a cart along the hallway.

"Excuse me, Mr. Morris," said Buster. "May I ask you a couple of questions?"

"Shoot."

Buster explained that he was trying to re-create the sequence of events from the previous afternoon.

" 'Sequence of events,' eh?" said Mr. Morris. "You sound like one of the those TV detective shows."

"Really?" said Buster. He beamed. Then he remembered that detectives don't beam and tried to look serious again.

"Tell me about yesterday."

"Well, let's see," said Mr. Morris. "I was in the teachers' room —"

"Aha!" said Buster suspiciously. "And *what* were you doing there?"

"Changing a lightbulb. Then I got the call to go to the kitchen. Seems Mrs. MacGrady was having some trouble with her mixer. When I got there, the floor was covered with brownie batter. So I cleaned up the mess."

Buster folded his arms. "And do you *always* clean up after Mrs. MacGrady?"

"No, not often. She's pretty tidy as a rule. But I was glad to help. Anything else?"

Buster wanted to think of more questions. He liked asking questions. But he couldn't think of any.

"Not at the moment. But do me a favor and don't leave town."

Mr. Morris smiled. "Whatever you say, Buster."

He gathered up his bucket and mop and started to walk away. With each step he made a jingling sound.

"Just a minute, Mr. Morris." Buster ran to catch up to him. "That jingling . . . It sounds like quarters. *A lot of quarters!*"

Mr. Morris pulled a huge key ring full of keys from his pocket. "I know what you mean," he said, jingling it. "I've often thought the same thing myself."

"Oh. Well, that's all right, then."

It wasn't really all right, thought Buster, at least not for Arthur. He had hoped to get to the bottom of the case quickly. But the more he dug, the more complicated the case became.

And the bottom was nowhere in sight.

Chapter 6

• • • • • • • • • • •

I had been on the job a couple of hours, but aside from one cherry tart, I had little to show for it. Nobody was calling the suspect a liar, but nobody could support his story, either. I thought maybe a change of scene would help, so I made my way to the suspect's home. There I met up with the suspect's sister. She seemed to be a pretty cool customer, but I knew I could handle her.

"Come on, D.W., you must know *something.*"

They were standing in the Reads' kitchen. Arthur had gone out for a while, D.W. had said. But he couldn't go far, she figured. The police were probably watching the train and bus stations. "And his pictures are probably on Wanted posters by now," she said.

"D.W., I'm trying to clear Arthur, not send him to jail. Now think hard."

D.W. made a face. "All right, all right, I'll tell you what I know."

"Go on." Buster got out his pad and pencil.

"Ready? Okay, take this down. Every single word."

Buster nodded.

"THAT . . . HAT . . . LOOKS . . . SILLY . . . ON . . . YOU."

Buster put down his pencil. "This is serious, D.W. Besides, I like the hat."

D.W. giggled.

"Now back to the subject at —"

"What is this, Buster, the third degree? If I knew anything, I'd certainly tell . . . well, maybe not you. But somebody."

Buster pushed back his fedora. "Don't try that smoke screen stuff on me. I can see through you like a window. Now, think back to yesterday. Did Arthur bring home any big jingling bags . . . you know, absentmindedly?"

D.W. glared at him. "Buster, you're talking about my brother! He would never take other people's money and bring it home like that."

"Calm down, D.W. I don't think Arthur would do anything bad on purpose. But he could have been forgetful. I'm just checking out every possibility."

"Arthur's not that stupid," D.W. went on. Clearly, she had been giving the matter some serious thought. "He wouldn't just bring the money into the house. Too many questions to answer. Too many people might see it. But he'd want it close by. Hidden. Safe. But where? That's what I can't quite figure out. Not that Arthur's so clever. But still . . ."

She scratched her head.

"Of course!" she shouted. "We should check the lawn for signs of recent digging."

"But D.W. —"

She ran out the door. But before Buster could follow her, Arthur walked in.

"Oh, Buster! I'm glad you're here. Does this mean good news?"

"Sorry, Arthur. The case is still wide open."

Arthur sighed.

"I'm just trying to be thorough," Buster explained. "Detectives need to be thorough."

"Buster, if you don't find out who did it by tomorrow, I'll miss the picnic."

"I know. I haven't —"

He hesitated as D.W. passed by, carrying a shovel.

"Excuse me. Step aside. Coming through."

Arthur stared at D.W. and started to say something, but Buster held up his hand.

"You're better off not asking," he said. "You really don't want to know."

Chapter 7

• • • • • • • • • • • •

The situation did not look good. Everything still pointed to just one person — Arthur. Could he really be a criminal mastermind? I tried to picture him in his secret hideout, swimming in a sea of shiny quarters. They dripped through his fingers as he laughed insanely. Quarters! Quarters! He could never get enough.

Dinner at the Baxter house was quiet that evening. Mrs. Baxter was used to hearing Buster talk all about his day. But tonight Buster was quiet. Too quiet.

"Are you feeling all right?" his mother asked.

Buster nodded.

"But you've only had two helpings of dessert. That's not like you, Buster. You're sure you don't have a headache or fever?"

Buster shook his head. "It's just this case, Mom. I haven't figured out how to help Arthur yet."

"You're a good friend, Buster. I'm sure Arthur appreciates that."

"I hope so." But right now, thought Buster, Arthur needs more than a good friend. He needs a good detective.

Later, Buster sat at his desk, flipping through his pad. He was looking for clues, any clues that would help him solve the case. He wasn't feeling picky, either. Big clues, small clues, ragged-round-the-edges clues — Buster would have happily accepted *any* of them.

The phone rang.

"Buster, it's for you."

It was the Brain. He wondered if Buster was having any luck.

"Not yet," Buster reported.

"Well, keep trying. If I think of anything, I'll call you back."

A few minutes later, the phone rang again. This time it was Francine.

"Any progress?" she asked.

"No," said Buster.

"Okay. Keep me informed."

He had barely put down the phone when it rang again. Now Muffy was on the line. "It's too bad we can't buy clues," she said. "That would make things so much easier."

Buster agreed. But clues just weren't for sale.

After that the phone was quiet. Buster lay on his bed as a swirl of images — Mrs. MacGrady, Mr. Morris, and Arthur —

passed by in his mind. They were all involved somehow. He just had to put the pieces of the puzzle together.

"Buster, it's getting late!"

"I'm trying to crack the case."

"Well, you need your sleep, Mr. Detective. You're not a robot."

"You're right, I'm not a . . ." Buster leapt to his feet. "Robot! That's it! Mom, I love you!"

He went to the phone and dialed Arthur.

"Hello?" said Arthur.

"Great news!" shouted Buster. "I figured it out!"

"Really?" Arthur got all excited. "So, tell me."

"Okay. Well, the quarters were stolen by an army of evil robots. They need the metal for fuel. Nobody noticed them because they can transform themselves into . . . into . . . any shape."

Arthur sighed. "That's it? That's your big breakthrough?"

"Gosh, it sounded a lot better a minute ago. . . ."

"You'd better get some sleep," said Arthur.

"Okay," said Buster. "You too."

"I'll try," said Arthur. But if his only chance depended on finding an army of robots, he figured he was in for a long night.

Chapter 8

• • • • • • • • • • • •

Detectives are supposed to be tough, but even they feel the pain when a friend is hurting. And it was no different for me. I could tell from Arthur's eyes that he was not happy. Actually, I could tell from his mouth, the slump of his shoulders, even his ears. Arthur was a mess.

"Are you sure you want to be seen with me?" Arthur asked on the way to school the next morning.

"Of course," said Buster.

"People might begin to think you're my partner in crime. You could be my accomplice, my henchman, my —"

"Arthur, stop! Listen, I would never desert you. I'm no rat leaving a sinking ship. Why, even if you went to jail, I would write you. I would come visit. Well, you know . . ."

Buster realized this wasn't helping much. "Anyway," he added, "I'm really sorry you're going to miss the picnic today. And it's because I'm a bad detective. I know you're innocent."

Arthur tried to smile. "Thanks, Buster."

"I hate letting you down. If I just had a little more time."

"Forget it," said Arthur. "You did your best. You might be a lousy detective —"

"*Bad*, Arthur. I said *bad*."

"Oh, right. You might be a bad detective, but you're still a good friend."

Buster and Arthur soon arrived at school. Buster got in line for the picnic bus with the other kids.

Mr. Ratburn motioned to Arthur.

"Sorry about this, Arthur."

"Me, too, Mr. Ratburn."

His teacher nodded. "Don't give up. I'm sure the truth will come out in the end."

Arthur certainly hoped so.

"Children!" Mr. Haney shouted through his bullhorn. "Please board the school bus now."

Buster was standing with Binky and the Brain. They started to move forward.

"Poor Arthur," said the Brain.

"A good lawyer could get him off," said Binky. "They do it all the time."

"But Arthur's innocent," said Buster. "I just don't know how to prove it. The answer's somewhere right in front of me. Hey, what's that?"

He pointed to Binky's shirt.

Binky looked down. "Powdered sugar, I guess. I had a doughnut on the way to school."

"Oh. See, that's a clue. If this was the case of the missing doughnuts, I'd be all set." Buster frowned. "I just can't think straight anymore."

"I know how you feel," said the Brain. "Sometimes when I'm working on a tough math problem, I feel like my brain's overflowing with data."

"Keep it moving," said Mr. Haney.

Buster stepped onto the bus. Suddenly he stopped and stared at the Brain.

"Overflowing? Overflowing!"

"I think the pressure got to him," Binky whispered.

"That's it!" cried Buster. He shook the Brain's hand. "That's it!"

"What's it?" said the Brain.

Buster raced off the bus and almost ran into Mr. Haney.

"Hold on there, Buster. You're going the wrong way."

"Mr. Haney! I've solved the crime. Come on!"

Without waiting for an answer, he led the way into the school.

Chapter 9

• • • • • • • • • • • •

Every detective wants to be cool, calm, and col-
lected at all times. And I was no different. But
it's easy to say that while you're sitting back in
your office with your feet up on the desk. It's
another thing when you think you've saved
your best friend from a fate worse than death.

In the kitchen, Mrs. MacGrady was
packing up for the school picnic. She had
the sandwiches, potato chips, and cartons
of juice all neatly organized on the counter.

She was just getting ready to cut the
sheet of brownies into squares when
Buster rushed in. He was pulling Mr.

Haney behind him. "Slow down, Buster," said Mr. Haney. "We don't want to be arrested for speeding."

Mrs. MacGrady looked surprised. "Buster! Mr. Haney! What are you doing here?"

Mr. Haney cleared his throat. "Following up on a theory. Go ahead, Buster."

"Mrs. MacGrady, do you know why your brownie mix overflowed?"

"Not really. I don't mind saying it was a little embarrassing. But Mr. Morris was very nice about helping me clean it up."

"Has that ever happened before? The overflowing, I mean."

"No. I'm always very careful. But this time I guess I made too much."

"Did you use a different recipe?"

Mrs. MacGrady stopped to think. "Well, no, now that you mention it. The recipe was the same as always."

"Did you use any new equipment?"

Mrs. MacGrady laughed. "Not on my budget. I'm lucky they give me electricity."

Mr. Haney cleared his throat.

Buster picked up a knife and cut a square out of the brownie pan.

"And yet somehow something happened, something that had never happened before. Significant, don't you think?"

Mr. Haney folded his arms. "Buster, make your point, please. The bus is waiting."

Buster was getting to it. But detectives never rush their moments of glory.

"So you measured out the ingredients in the usual way. And you mixed them in the usual way. And yet something unusual happened. Shall I tell you why?"

Mrs. MacGrady smiled. "Please do."

"It's because you accidentally included one extra ingredient."

"I did?"

Buster nodded. He picked up the brownie and broke it in two.

A quarter fell out.

"Oh, my," said Mrs. MacGrady. "How did that happen?"

"It was Arthur," Buster explained. "You were on the phone when he came in. He thought you saw him, but you didn't. Then he left the bag of quarters next to the other ingredients. He had even spilled some of your flour on his bag, which is probably why you didn't notice."

Mrs. MacGrady broke open another brownie, and two quarters fell out.

"So now we know the truth," said Mr. Haney.

"Arthur is innocent!" Buster exclaimed. "It's time to set him free."

Chapter 10

● ● ● ● ● ● ● ● ● ● ● ● ●

One kind of detective fades back into the shadows once a case is solved. For that detective, solving the mystery is its own reward. He dodges the bright lights of the television cameras and the front page of the newspaper.

The other kind of detective likes to take a bow, to be recognized for doing good work. He doesn't duck the well-deserved compliment. I could see both sides, and I understood that some detectives would be shy about taking credit for untangling things.

But I wasn't one of them.

Arthur was sitting in detention alone with his thoughts. And at that particular moment, his thoughts were not very good company. The quarters were gone, and his reputation was in question. Even if he was someday proved innocent, he was still going to miss the third-grade picnic.

He could hear Miss Tingley typing in the next room. The clicking on the keyboard made Arthur think of crickets chirping. At least crickets were free to do what they wanted. They didn't have to worry about quarters or picnics or unexpected mysteries.

Suddenly Arthur heard another noise. This didn't sound like crickets at all. It sounded like *a lot* of people on the move.

Miss Tingley heard it, too. She stopped typing and got up to see what all the commotion was about.

It *was* a lot of people. The whole third

grade was coming down the hall. The students, the teachers, and even the bus driver were there.

"What's going on?" Miss Tingley asked.

"Stand back," Mr. Haney advised her. He opened the door to the room where Arthur was sitting. "Justice is about to be served."

"Arthur, I did it!" shouted Buster. "You're free."

Arthur stood up.

"I am? But how?"

"We've solved the mystery of the missing quarters," Mr. Haney explained. "They ended up in Mrs. MacGrady's brownies."

"Really?" said Arthur. He looked at Mr. Ratburn, who smiled at him.

"They must be the richest brownies she's ever made," said the Brain.

Everyone laughed.

"And," said Buster, "you owe it all to that great detective, that peerless investigator —"

Buster was cut off as Mr. Haney spoke into the bullhorn.

"Back to the bus, everyone!" he ordered. "The picnic awaits."

As the kids went back outside, Arthur shook Buster's hand.

"Thanks, Buster. I'm almost speechless. You're the best detective I know!"

"I'm the *only* detective you know."

"Well, yes, but you're still the best."

"If you say so."

"I do."

"All right."

He went on like that all the way out to the bus. I didn't try to stop him. A good detective knows when to sit back and listen.

The picnic was a big success. Later, though, Mrs. MacGrady faced a new mystery when a

plate of cookies she had put aside suddenly disappeared.

I brushed a few crumbs off my shirt and joined in the baseball game that was starting up. If Mrs. MacGrady wanted to solve that mystery, she was going to have to do it on her own.

Locked in the
Library!

Chapter 1

● ● ● ● ● ● ● ● ● ● ●

Arthur and Buster were walking up the school steps one morning when an angry voice shouted behind them, "ARTHUR! ARTHUR READ!"

Arthur turned.

Buster turned, too.

The voice belonged to Francine. She was charging toward them. Muffy and Sue Ellen were with her.

"What's up?" asked Arthur.

Francine folded her arms. "I'll tell you what's up. You told everyone I looked like a marshmallow."

"I did?"

Buster nodded. "Don't you remember, Arthur? She was wearing that goofy sweater, the one that puffs up everywhere."

"Oh, *that* sweater." Arthur remembered it now. It had padded shoulders and wool that fluffed out like frosting.

"You'd better say you're sorry," said Francine.

"Or what?" said Buster.

Francine ignored Buster and stared Arthur in the eye.

"Or else you're going to get it."

"Oh, yeah?" said Buster. "You can't talk to Arthur that way."

Francine tossed her head and continued up the steps.

Muffy and Sue Ellen did the same.

"I guess we told *them*," said Buster.

" 'We'?" said Arthur.

"You don't have to thank me," said

Buster, putting his arm around Arthur's shoulders. "That's what friends are for."

Arthur just sighed.

A little while later, when he went into class, he could feel himself being glared at.

"This is all your fault," he said to Buster.

Buster wedged himself into Arthur's seat. "*My* fault?" he said. "You're the one who called Francine a marshmallow."

"And you're the one who talked so tough."

"I was just standing up for you."

"I think it might be better if I stood up for myself."

A folded note flew through the air and landed on Arthur's desk. He unfolded it and read it aloud quietly.

"*This is your final warning. You are —*"

Buster grabbed the note out of Arthur's hand.

"*. . . in big trouble,*" he continued. "*And I*

mean BIG." He paused. "I think that's a skull and crossbones." He stopped to think. "That's not a good sign."

Arthur turned around and looked at Francine. She was still glaring at him. Muffy and Sue Ellen were glaring at him, too.

"Attention, please!" said the teacher, Mr. Ratburn, from the front of the room. "Buster, perhaps you would consider taking your own seat."

Buster pulled himself out of Arthur's chair and zipped back to his own.

"Now," Mr. Ratburn continued, standing at the blackboard, "let's get started. Have you ever wondered what makes a hero or heroine? Are people born brave and generous, or do they become this way later on?"

The kids all looked at one another. They were puzzled. Were they supposed to answer the question, or was Mr. Ratburn just talking to himself? He did that sometimes.

"Anyway," Mr. Ratburn went on, "that's what I want you to think about this weekend."

Everyone groaned.

"Please prepare an oral report on the hero or heroine of your choice. You'll be working in pairs." Mr. Ratburn consulted his notes. "Binky, you're with Sue Ellen. Muffy, you'll be working with Buster." He named some other pairs. "And Arthur, you're teamed with Francine."

Arthur glanced at Francine. She looked like she was going to die.

He sighed. It was going to be a very long weekend.

Chapter 2

Heroes and heroines. That's what Arthur and Buster talked about on their way home from school.

"Who's your favorite?" Buster asked. "I mean, there are a lot of heroes to choose from. I know we're studying the ones from real life. But what about Robin Hood or Hercules?"

"Or the Bionic Bunny," said Arthur.

Buster nodded. "Exactly," he said.

Arthur wasn't sure he had a favorite. He had always liked reading stories about heroes, but he had never thought much about what made them the way they were or which ones he liked best.

"You know what I really like about heroes?" said Buster.

"What?"

"Well, that they're so heroic, so brave. I wish I could do half the things they do."

"Me, too," said Arthur. He paused. "Do you think heroes ever call their friends marshmallows?"

Buster wasn't sure. "I know one thing. If they do, they don't worry about it later."

Arthur nodded. It would certainly help things if he could be a little more heroic himself.

When Arthur got home, he found D.W. talking on the kitchen phone.

"He said *what?*" D.W. gasped.

She listened for a moment.

"I can't believe it," she went on. "Well, I

suppose I can. Nothing Arthur does really surprises me."

She glared at her brother.

Arthur shook his head. He was being glared at a lot lately.

"Who are you talking to?" he asked.

D.W. ignored him. "Uh-huh . . . Well, he should talk. Guess what he looks like in his pajamas? . . . No . . . No, but I like that one. Give up?"

"D.W.!" Arthur shouted.

"A dumpling. He looks like a soggy dumpling."

Arthur reached for the phone.

D.W. held up her hand to stop him. "Okay," she said. "I'll tell him. Bye."

She hung up the phone.

"Wasn't that for me?" said Arthur.

"Yes and no." D.W. smiled. "I have to give you the message because Francine isn't talking to you."

"She's not?"

D.W. laughed. "You can't go around calling someone a marshmallow and expect her not to care."

"I didn't know it was such a big deal," said Arthur. "I mean, I like marshmallows."

D.W. was not impressed. "To eat, maybe, but not to look like."

Arthur rolled his eyes. "So what was the message?" he asked.

"Francine says to meet her at the library tomorrow at three. But you can't speak to her because she's not speaking to you."

Arthur sighed.

D.W. stuck her nose in the air. "And I don't blame her."

"But how are we supposed to get any work done if we're not speaking?"

D.W. wagged her finger at him. "You should have thought of that before you started calling people names."

And with that, D.W. went upstairs, leaving Arthur thinking that if he were a hero, he wouldn't be in this mess.

Chapter 3

• • • • • • • • • • • •

The next afternoon, Arthur ran up the steps of the Elwood City library just as the clock struck three.

Phew, he thought.

He had been playing in the backyard with Pal and had lost track of the time. So he had needed to hurry. If Francine had to wait for him, that would just give her something else to complain about.

Inside the library, Arthur saw the librarian, Ms. Turner, standing by the reference desk. Francine was with her.

"Hello, Ms. Turner," he said.

The librarian looked up from the book she was consulting. She smiled.

"Good afternoon, Arthur. Francine was just telling me about your report."

Arthur had hoped that Francine might have used up her glare by now. But as she turned toward him, he could see that it was still going strong.

"As I was saying," said Francine, "even though we're working on this report together, I'm in charge."

"Oh, really?" said Arthur. "I don't remember Mr. Ratburn saying anything about that."

Francine folded her arms. "Well, you just weren't listening closely enough. Probably too busy thinking up new insults."

"I was not!"

Francine turned away. "Of course, we're not going to discuss it further, because we're not speaking to each other."

"Francine, that's the most —"

"Heroes can be so inspirational," Ms. Turner put in. "Don't you agree, Arthur? Francine was just telling me some of her ideas. What sort of hero are you looking for?"

"Well," said Arthur, trying to get himself under control. "Let's see. Someone heroic, of course."

"Ooooh!" said Francine. "Good thought, Arthur."

Arthur turned a little red. "I'm just thinking out loud. He might be —"

"What about a *she?*" said Francine.

"Okay," said Arthur. "A woman is fine as long as she did something famous."

Ms. Turner tapped her pencil on the counter. "How about Joan of Arc?" she said. "She was certainly famous, and one of the youngest leaders in history. She was an inspiration, leading the French army in battle against the English invaders. Her story has battles, horses — exciting stuff. I believe we have books about her in the European History section as well as in the biographies."

"I'll take biographies," Arthur and Francine said together.

They stared at each other.

"I called it first!" said Francine.

"You did not!"

"Did, too!"

"Goodness, children," said Ms. Turner. "It's nice to see such enthusiasm." She looked at their frowning faces. "But maybe I should decide. Francine, you were here first, so why don't you look in the biographies."

"Yes!" said Francine. She stuck out her tongue at Arthur.

"As for you, Arthur, you could try the stacks. Medieval French history is in the 940s. That's down the stairs and around the corner."

Arthur nodded.

Francine headed down the aisle.

"But don't forget," Ms. Turner called after them, "the library will close promptly at—"

"We know," said Francine. "Five o'clock."

Chapter 4

• • • • • • • • • • • •

Arthur found a big book on French history at 940.21. He was impressed that Ms. Turner knew just where to send him without looking anything up. The library number system was confusing to him.

The book had a tapestry on the front, decorated with unicorns and women in long dresses. Inside, Arthur found a lot of information. Some of the French had conquered England in 1066, but by the early 1400s, much of France was under English control.

And the French didn't like that.

Holding the book in both hands, Arthur

settled onto a big, comfortable couch next to a grandfather clock. Then he started to read. There were tons of facts to get through. Before long, his eyelids grew heavy, and he slumped down against the cushion.

"Look out, Sir Arthur!" cried a voice from the battlement.

Arthur ducked as an arrow whizzed harmlessly over his head.

"Thank you, Lord Buster!" he called out.

"We are lucky the French have such poor aim," said Lord Buster.

"True," said Sir Arthur. "But I fear they plan to do a lot of practicing."

From his perch, Arthur looked out over the field of battle. The French army had gathered in great force outside the moat.

Sir Arthur shook his head. All this had happened just because he had called the French general a marshmallow. She had taken great offense at that.

He regretted the comment now, but he was too proud to admit it. Besides, the French general didn't seem in the mood for apologies.

She was riding her horse back and forth in front of her troops.

"We will take the castle!" she was saying in French — although Arthur could somehow understand her.

Her army cheered.

"Then we will see who is the marshmallow around here."

Arthur heard the clock in the tower ringing out the hour. Bong, bong, bong, bong, bong. The day was growing late. Did the French still plan to attack — or would they wait until morning?

Up the stairs and around the corner, Francine had opened a chapter book about

Joan of Arc. It was nice and private here. As long as she stayed put, she wouldn't have to risk running into Arthur.

Francine sat down cross-legged and put on her Walkman. She had brought a tape to play while she read. That way, even if Arthur found her, she could easily ignore him.

The book itself was pretty interesting. It told of how Joan of Arc led the French army and defeated the English at Orléans. The Maid of Orléans, she was called. She was only about seventeen when she started fighting, but she got to wear armor and carry a sword.

Francine wondered about the armor. It must have been heavy. If Joan ever fell down, did she need help getting up?

Humming to the music, she kept reading as the light faded in the windows at the end of the aisle.

Chapter 5

• • • • • • • • • • •

Arthur yawned. He hadn't meant to fall asleep. The nap had just sneaked up on him. He stretched lazily. He had never thought of the library as a good place to sleep, but it certainly was quiet.

He stood up and walked back toward the main desk. The only sound he heard was his own footsteps. That seemed odd. The library was supposed to be quiet, of course, but this seemed *too quiet.*

"Ms. Turner?" Arthur called out.

Nobody answered.

Arthur looked around. A lot of the lights

were off. That was odd, too. He ran to the front door and pulled the handle.

The door was locked! Arthur shook it as hard as he could.

The door stayed locked.

Suddenly the grandfather clock began to chime.

Bong, bong, bong, bong, bong, bong!

Arthur was counting. Six bongs! That meant six o'clock. But the library closed at five. He distinctly remembered Ms. Turner mentioning that fact. That meant the library was . . . closed!

Arthur was scared. How could the library be closed? He was still inside it. Libraries weren't supposed to close with people inside them.

Arthur gulped. If he was inside by himself, that meant he was alone. Very alone.

Suddenly the library's familiar nooks

and crannies didn't look so friendly. Were those shadows moving across the floor to grab him? No, no, they were just the shadows of branches blown by the wind. What about the books, though? If he turned his back on them, would they fly off the shelves and hit him in the back?

Arthur squeezed his eyes shut. Stay calm, he told himself. It's only a library.

He opened one eye to take another look. Everything seemed normal. He opened the other. The shadows were minding their own business. The books hadn't moved from the stacks.

Crassshhh!

Arthur jumped. That sound was not his imagination. His imagination couldn't make up a noise like that.

Arthur bit his lip. Maybe he wasn't alone in the library. The thought should have made him feel better — but it didn't.

"Hello? Is anyone there?"

No one answered. Arthur walked along, looking around. Someone or something had made that crash. He had to find out more.

With his heart pounding in his chest, he took a few steps forward. He tried to walk silently, but the floor creaked under his sneakers.

When he reached the stairs, Arthur looked up and down the stairwell. Both directions looked dark and scary.

What would Joan of Arc have done in this situation? Arthur wondered. She at least would have been armed for battle. The only thing Arthur had to protect himself with was a pencil — and even that needed sharpening.

Arthur listened carefully. There had been no further crashes. Maybe the first one was a fluke, a pile of books that had

fallen over. Maybe he could relax a little —
and concentrate on getting out of the
library.

And then a hand grabbed his shoulder
from behind.

Chapter 6

. . . .

"Aagghh!" Arthur screamed. He whirled around.

"Aagghh!" Francine screamed back. She was standing right behind him.

The two of them just stood there, shaking for a moment.

"Why did you scream?" she cried.

"You screamed, too," said Arthur.

"Only because you screamed first."

Arthur took a deep breath. "Well, why shouldn't I scream? I'm alone in a dark library. I hear a crash—"

"That wasn't a crash," said Francine. "I

accidentally knocked some books off a desk. It barely made any noise at all."

"It sounded like a crash to me," Arthur insisted. "And then I go to investigate, and this creepy hand grabs me on the shoulder—"

"My hand isn't creepy," said Francine. "It's a very nice hand." She looked at it and smiled. Then her smile turned to a frown. "Anyway, what are you doing here?"

Arthur put his hands on his hips. "I could ask you the same question," he said.

Francine sighed. "I was looking for Ms. Turner. Then I heard the clock chiming. It's after six, you know."

"I can count, Francine."

She was not impressed. "So you say. But where were you an hour ago?"

"Looking through some books."

"Well, why didn't you come find me?

The library was closing. Five o'clock, remember? You got us locked in."

Arthur blushed. "I did not!"

"So then what happened?"

Arthur hesitated. "Well, actually, I fell asleep."

"Asleep!" Francine laughed. "You must feel pretty silly."

Arthur made a face. "Maybe I do, and maybe I don't. But at least I have an excuse. What about you? Since you remember the time so well, why didn't you come find *me*?"

Now it was Francine's turn to blush. "Okay, okay, I was listening to music while I looked through the books. I guess I didn't hear the clock, either."

"Ha! So you weren't paying any more attention than I was."

"Never mind that," said Francine. "I don't have time to argue with you. I have to get out of here."

"Fine," said Arthur. "Do you have a plan?"

"A plan?"

"A way to get out." Arthur frowned. "As you said, we're locked in."

"I'm working on one," she sniffed. "And when it's ready, I'll put it into operation. But I'm not going to share my ideas with you. Do you know why? Because I'm still not talking to you. And I'm not listening, either."

To make the point perfectly clear, Francine stuck her fingers in her ears and walked away.

Chapter 7

● ● ● ● ● ● ● ● ● ● ● ●

Even though Arthur and Francine were not working together, they both had the same idea about what to do next.

Maybe I can climb out a window, thought Arthur.

I think I'll try the window, thought Francine.

Arthur began piling up a rickety pile of books. When he was done, he began climbing up.

The pile swayed back and forth.

Arthur was about to grab the window handle when Francine came by. One of the books in Arthur's pile was exactly the size she needed to complete a nice, neat pile of her own.

She yanked out the book.

Arthur's pile fell down. Arthur hit the floor with a loud thud.

"You should build things more carefully," said Francine.

With the last book in place, Francine's pile was perfectly steady. She climbed up to the window and gave the latch a pull.

It was stuck.

She gave it a few tugs, but the latch didn't move.

A fly buzzed in front of her face.

"Go away!" said Francine. "Find your own way out."

She waved her hand wildly at the fly.

"Whoaaaa!" Francine landed with a crash.

Arthur came running around the corner and almost tripped over Francine, who was lying on the floor.

"What happened?" he asked.

Francine picked herself up. "I lost my balance," she said, forgetting that she wasn't talking to him.

"What about the window?"

Francine shook her head. "Forget it," she said. "I don't think these windows have been opened in a long time."

"Uh-oh!"

"What?" Francine snapped.

"I just remembered something," said Arthur. "Today is Saturday. That means the library is closed until—"

"Monday!" Francine finished for him. She gulped. "What's that noise?"

"What noise?"

"I hear growling."

Arthur looked down. "That's my stomach. It's thinking about getting no food for the entire weekend."

"We have more than your stomach to

worry about," said Francine. "Our families will be worried sick."

Arthur thought about how D.W. would take the news. He could picture her pulling down his posters, throwing out his toys, and painting the walls pink.

"Not everyone," he said.

"Wait a minute!" said Francine. "I've got it."

She ran to the card catalog and began flipping through the listings.

"Are you crazy?" said Arthur. "How is a *book* going to help us?"

Francine ignored him. "Let's see," she said. *"How to Escape from Prison, How to Escape from a Desert Island* . . . Aha!"

"Aha, what?" said Arthur.

"How to Escape from a Library, of course."

Arthur was impressed. He hadn't realized that this sort of thing happened so often.

"Hey! Wait for me!" he said, following Francine into the stacks.

She found the place for the book. It made a hole like the gap in a smile after a tooth has fallen out.

"I don't believe it! Who would need a book on escaping from a library unless they were already *in* a library? And if someone was here with us"—she looked around — "I guess we would know about it."

"So, now what?" said Arthur.

Francine sighed. "I wish I knew."

Chapter 8

The library had seemed dark before. Now somehow it seemed even darker. The rooms had seemed silent before. Now they seemed almost frozen in quiet.

Rinnggg!

"What's that?" asked Francine. She looked at Arthur.

"PHONE!" they said together.

They raced back to the main desk. The phone was still ringing.

Francine grabbed the receiver.

"Hello?"

"Hello, Ms. Turner," said the voice on the

line. *"This is Muffy Crosswire. I didn't get a chance to —"*

"Muffy!" Francine cut in. "It's me, Francine. Listen, I'm locked—"

"Oh, sorry, Francine, I must have dialed you by mistake. I meant to call the library. Ooops, can't talk now. I hear the bell for dinner. I'll talk to you later. Bye."

She hung up.

"Muffy! Wait! Muffy?" Francine stared at the phone.

"What did you do?" Arthur shouted. "How could you hang up on her?"

"I didn't hang up on her. She hung up on me. Anyway, I'm calling my mother, so relax."

Francine dialed her home number. She heard a *beep* and then a recording.

"We're sorry. To dial out of the library, you must enter the correct user code. Please hang up and try again."

"User code?" Francine stared at the phone. "But I don't know the user code."

She tried again anyway.

"We're sorry. To dial out of the library, you must enter —"

Francine slammed down the phone. "User codes! Passwords! What's this world coming to, anyway?"

"We're doomed," said Arthur.

"Oh, Arthur, just relax. You're such a wimp."

"Me? Well, you're a bossy, know-it-all . . . marshmallow."

"That does it, Arthur Read! If I have to spend the weekend here, I'm not spending it with you!"

She stormed out of the room.

"Fine with me," Arthur called after her. He looked around at the deepening gloom. "See if I care," he added softly.

Left to himself, Arthur looked around

for something to do. He picked up a magazine and started flipping through it. There was a picture of a roast turkey on one page.

Arthur's stomach grumbled.

"That sure looks good," he muttered. He ripped off part of the page and tried chewing it.

"Yuck!" he said, spitting it out. It didn't taste like turkey at all.

Thump!

What was that?

Thump!

Arthur frowned. Libraries were not supposed to make thumping noises.

"Francine?"

She didn't answer.

Arthur went back to the magazine. He wondered if the mashed potatoes and gravy would taste any better than the turkey leg.

Thump!

Arthur put down the magazine.

"Francine!" he called out.

The name echoed through the halls.

Where was she? Arthur started moving in the direction that Francine had gone.

"Francine! Francine! Where are you?"

Thump!

There it was again. And this time he also heard a girl screaming.

"Francine! Don't worry! I'm coming."

Arthur ran up the steps to the next level. He threw open the first door he came to.

It was a broom closet.

Arthur kept going. He heard more screaming coming from another door down the hall.

Arthur raced toward the door. He heard evil laughter coming from the other side.

There was no time to waste. Francine was in trouble! He took a deep breath — and burst in.

Chapter 9

●●●●●●●●●●●

As he entered the room, Arthur tripped on the rug and fell to the floor. His glasses flew off and sailed across the room.

They landed in the middle of a pizza box.

Arthur squinted and looked around.

"Francine, are you okay?"

Francine was sitting in a chair watching television.

"Of course I'm okay. Why wouldn't I be?"

Arthur scrambled across the floor and picked up his glasses. Strands of cheese dangled from the lenses.

Arthur wiped them off and put the glasses back on.

"I wasn't sure," he said. "I heard thumping."

"Oh, that . . . The movie I'm watching has monsters with big feet."

"And screaming!"

"Naturally. It's a horror movie."

"And evil laughing," Arthur went on.

"I know," said Francine. "The monsters have a strange sense of humor."

"So do you!" said Arthur. "When you didn't answer, I figured you were hurt or something. I was worried. I was coming to your rescue." He looked around. "Where are we, anyway?"

Francine shrugged. "It's the staff room, I think. I had no idea librarians were so well fed. I found the pizza in the refrigerator and zapped it in the microwave."

"Francine, let me get this straight. We're locked in the library. It's getting dark. We don't know how long we're going to be stuck here. And you're sitting here eating pizza and watching TV?"

She nodded. "I'll bet you had no idea I could be so resourceful."

That was true, but Arthur wasn't about to admit it. "Well, I only have one thing to say."

"And what's that?"

Arthur's stomach grumbled. "Were you planning to share?"

Francine considered it. "Why should I share with someone who calls me a marshmallow?"

"Look who's talking. You've got a pretty short memory. Remember when I got glasses? You called me four-eyes."

"Well, I . . . That's ancient history." She paused. "Hey, did you say you were coming to my rescue?"

"Sort of."

"You were, weren't you?" Francine

picked up another plate. "That was very brave of you, Arthur. Joan of Arc would be pleased." She paused. "Want some pizza?"

"Sure."

A little while later, Arthur and Francine sat back in their chairs.

"Ohhhh!" Arthur groaned.

"Double ohhhh!" said Francine.

The pizza was gone, and several empty packages of chips and cookies were scattered around.

Arthur smiled. "This is turning out better than I expected. No chores, no homework, no . . . D.W!"

He sat up in horror. His sister D.W. had suddenly appeared in the doorway.

"Hello, Arthur," she said. "You're in *big* trouble."

Just then, Arthur's father and Francine's mother came around the corner. Ms. Turner was with them.

"Arthur! Francine!" said Mr. Read.

"Thank goodness you're all right!" said Mrs. Frensky.

Ms. Turner shook her head. "I don't know how this could have happened. But I'm glad to see both of you children."

"Are you all right?" asked Mr. Read.

"Are you hurt?" asked Mrs. Frensky.

D.W. took a look around at the chips, the cookies, and the empty pizza box.

"Don't worry," she said. "I think they'll survive."

Chapter 10

• • • • • • • • • • • •

Monday morning at school, everyone was crowding around to hear the full story.

"I've always thought," said Binky, "that the characters in books come out to play after the library closes. I don't suppose you saw any."

"Of course not," said Francine. "They're afraid of the ghosts."

"Ghosts!" said Buster. He shivered a little.

Francine nodded. "But they didn't bother us."

"Except for that one with no head," said Arthur. "Right, Francine?"

They winked at each other.

As the bell rang, the kids headed for their classrooms.

"So, who'd you do your report on?" Buster asked Arthur.

Arthur stopped short. Francine would have bumped into him, but she had stopped short, too.

"Report?"

Arthur and Francine exchanged a panicky look. In all the excitement, they had forgotten about Joan of Arc.

That look was still on their faces as Muffy finished her report a little while later. The blackboard was lined with Crosswire Motors charts and graphs.

"And so," she concluded, "it is no exaggeration to say that without Edward M. Crosswire, there would be no Elwood City as we know it."

"Very, um, illuminating, Muffy," said Mr. Ratburn. "That brings us to"— he looked down at his notes — "Arthur and Francine."

The two partners shuffled up to the front of the room. They stood before the class and cleared their throats.

"Um," said Arthur, "we picked Joan of Arc for our report. But we really didn't get a chance to learn as much as we could . . ."

"Because," Francine said suddenly, "we were too busy learning the true meaning of heroism. It isn't just the stuff you find in books. It's real life."

Arthur stared at her.

"That's right," Francine went on. "When we were locked in the library, it might have been really terrible. Actually, it was terrible at first, because we were fighting and everything. Then Arthur came to rescue me because he thought I was in danger."

"Exactly," said Arthur. "And Francine was really brave and resourceful, too. She found out where the food was. And saved me some pizza."

The class cheered.

"That's very good," said Mr. Ratburn. "It looks like your adventure taught you something important."

Arthur and Francine beamed at each other.

"So I'll give you until tomorrow to do your assignment."

"After all we've been through?" said Francine.

"Oh, yes," said Mr. Ratburn. "It should give your report special meaning."

Later that day, Arthur and Buster were walking home from school.

"I hate to say it," said Buster, "but Francine's not so bad."

Arthur nodded. "She can be a lot of fun. She's a good friend."

At that moment, Francine whizzed by

on her bike. She rode right through a puddle, splattering the boys with muddy water.

"Sorrryyy!" she yelled over her shoulder.

Arthur and Buster looked down at their wet shirts.

Arthur sighed. "But nobody's perfect," he said.

Marc Brown is the creator of the best-selling Arthur Adventure book series and codeveloper of the number one children's PBS television series, *Arthur*. He has also created a second book series, featuring D.W., Arthur's little sister, as well as numerous other books for children. Marc Brown lives with his family in Hingham, Massachusetts, and on Martha's Vineyard.

• • • • • • • • • •